Ian Livingst[one]
Adventures of Goldhawk

Darkmoon's Curse

Y0-CCL-847

PUFFIN BOOKS

PUFFIN BOOKS

Published by the Penguin Group
Penguin Books Ltd, 27 Wrights Lane, London W8 5TZ, England
Penguin Books USA Inc., 375 Hudson Street, New York, New York 10014, USA
Penguin Books Australia Ltd, Ringwood, Victoria, Australia
Penguin Books Canada Ltd, 10 Alcorn Avenue, Toronto, Ontario, Canada M4V 3B2
Penguin Books (NZ) Ltd, 182–190 Wairau Road, Auckland 10, New Zealand

Penguin Books Ltd, Registered Offices: Harmondsworth, Middlesex, England

First published 1995
10 9 8 7 6 5 4 3 2 1

Fighting Fantasy concept copyright © Steve Jackson and Ian Livingstone
Adventures of Goldhawk concept copyright © Ian Livingstone, 1995
Text copyright © Ian Livingstone, 1995
Illustrations copyright © Russ Nicholson, 1995
All rights reserved

The moral right of the author has been asserted

Reproduction by Anglia Graphics Ltd, Bedford
Printed in Great Britain by William Clowes Limited, Beccles and London

Filmset in Palatino

Except in the United States of America, this book is sold subject to the condition that it shall not, by
way of trade or otherwise, be lent, re-sold, hired out, or otherwise circulated without the publisher's
prior consent in any form of binding or cover other than that in which it is published and without a
similar condition including this condition being imposed on the subsequent purchaser.

The TERRIBLE WAR BETWEEN THE PEOPLE OF Karazan and the Orcs has been going on for two long and weary years. The Karazan army has been in retreat for nearly a week, ever since the King was slain on the battlefield and his ancient crown was taken by a gloating Orc General to Maggot Manor to be given to the chaos wizard, Darkmoon, the most evil enemy of Karazan.

In Karazan Castle, young Prince Goldhawk is being made ready to become the new King, but ancient lore decrees that the crown must be used in the ceremony. A plan has been hastily drawn up: Orlando, Goldhawk's Dwarf servant, has been sent on a secret mission to get the crown back from Darkmoon.

Orlando has been gone only a day when disaster strikes again. The Orcs have secretly sent an assassin into Karazan Castle to poison Prince Goldhawk; he would have succeeded but for the swift action of Marris, the old wizard of the court. Last night, during dinner, the Prince slumped forward, unconscious, after a single spoonful of soup, and Marris quickly gave him a potion of healing. During the commotion, the assassin slipped, unnoticed, out of the castle.

It is now the following morning and Marris has been up all night looking after the Prince, who is still unconscious. Suddenly there is a knock at the Prince's bedroom door ...

`Come in!' Marris says sharply.

The door opens and a tall man in shining armour strides quickly into the room, his footsteps tapping loudly on the polished stone floor. He approaches Marris with a worried look on his face.

`It's Orlando, sir. He has returned, but he's no longer a dwarf.'

`What!' Marris shouts. `Not a Dwarf? *Not a Dwarf?* What is he then? Explain yourself – and quickly!'

`He's been turned into a strange, metallic creature by Darkmoon. He's become a Tin Pig – although he can still speak,' the guard replies.

`Well, send him in, then!'

The guard retreats quickly from the room, and a few moments later a small creature with a large snout and long, pointed ears shuffles into the room. Its round body is covered with shiny, tin-like plates that make it look like a cross between an armadillo and a pig.

`Hello, Marris. It's me, Orlando,' the small creature says in a sad voice, `I'm afraid I've got myself into a terrible mess, oh yes, oh yes.'

Orlando suddenly catches sight of the Prince, and Marris explains how the assassin almost succeeded in killing Goldhawk.

`But you had better tell me what has happened to you,' Marris goes on.

`Well, at first everything went according to plan. I reached Maggot Manor safely, I found my way through Darkmoon's maze until I finally reached the poisonous herb garden outside his chambers ... only to spring a simple rope trap. I was flung up into the air by one leg and found myself bobbing helplessly, upside down, from a high branch of a tree.

`It wasn't long before Darkmoon appeared. He had on long black robes that trailed behind him as he walked, shoulders hunched, and he was rubbing his hands together gleefully. He had long black fingernails – not a very pleasant sight at all,' Orlando said glumly.

`He looked up at me and sneered, ``Ah, a little round man has come to visit me. I think I've caught myself a thief. Now, my little friend, you must pay for your foolishness.''

`Just then, I heard a loud buzzing sound, and Darkmoon froze like a statue. A plump dragonfly was hovering, a little way above his head. Darkmoon's jaw dropped

slowly open – then suddenly a long, sticky tongue uncoiled from his mouth and caught the dragonfly in mid-air. As he munched away he said, ``Mmm, purple dragonflies, my favourite. Now where was I? Ah, yes, I remember, I was about to punish this dangling Dwarf.''

`By now I was very scared, and if I wriggled it only tightened the rope round my ankle. Darkmoon reached into his robes and took out a large glass jar full of green paste and said, ``I've got some lovely medicine for you. It's made of crushed slugs, centipedes' legs, rats' tails, poopoo berries, sour gunk milk, scabweed, lardifat, dried niff leaf and a few drops of frog spittle. Now, doesn't that sound yummy? It will make you as strong as ten oxen.'' Then he lifted both hands towards me, one with the palm facing me and the other with the palm away from me. ``True or false?'' he said.

` ``False,'' I replied rather meekly.

` ``Correct!'' he shouted, hardly able to control himself.

``Now ... open wide ... dear Dwarf or, I'll let the spotted

drilibill birds feed on you! What's it to be then?"

`What a choice! I opened my mouth and grimaced while that ugly wizard fed me the foul-tasting goo. Minutes later, I fell into a deep sleep. When I woke up, I found myself in a field of long grass – and I couldn't believe what had happened to me! Instead of looking down at my fat but friendly stomach, I was horrified to see four little trotters, pointing at the sky. I rolled over and stood up, and then I ran round and round in a circle, squealing at the top of my voice.'

`So what did you do?' Marris asks eagerly.

`Eventually I calmed down. I tried to look on the bright side. I found that I could roll myself up into a ball – a cannonball, I suppose – so I could bowl my enemies over like skittles. And soon I found out that I also had a much keener sense of smell because my snout is so sensitive, although this is a mixed blessing – depending on the company I am in! All in all, it could have been worse.'

`Well, I'm very pleased you have returned, Orlando, but now we are in even greater peril. The King is dead, the Prince lies unconscious and that evil wizard Darkmoon has our crown. We need our Prince alive to show to our people and the Orcs that we can fight on! But who knows when the Prince will recover. The poison he was given was strong.'

Marris paces up and down the bedroom, rubbing his chin thoughtfully. Suddenly he claps his hands.

`I've got it: we'll open the Time Gate!' he says excitedly. `We'll find a new Prince from a far off time to help us.' Marris rushes out of the bedroom. Minutes later he returns, carrying a red box which he places on Goldhawk's bed. Orlando watches, amazed, as Marris opens the box. An arc of light crackles noisily round the unconscious Prince.

Marris utters a secret spell, and the light dies away.

`It's done,' Marris says softly. `Now we must wait.'

At the very moment when the Time Gate is opened, YOU are at home, lying in bed and reading a book about a magical kingdom called Karazan. Suddenly, an arc of light shoots through the window. It covers you completely, and then the room starts to spin. Everything goes blank and you feel as if you are falling through space and time.

In your mind, you land with a bump on a very hard floor and you open your eyes. You are standing in a large, stone-walled room which is lit by candles. There is a big four-poster bed at one end and a young man is lying on it, asleep. An old man wearing long robes is watching you with a smile on his face, and behind him stands a strange, pig-like creature. You realize that you must be looking at Prince Goldhawk, Marris and Orlando.

`Welcome to Karazan, young adventurer,' Marris says. `I think you know why you are here. You are our new Prince

Goldhawk! We are honoured that you will help us.'

You can hardly believe what is happening – surely you must be dreaming! But no, it is true. You look in a mirror on the bedroom wall and see that you do indeed look like the Prince. Your features must have altered when you passed through the Time Gate.

`But...but...well, I suppose,' you begin, when Marris slaps you on the back.

`Good!' he shouts and leads you into another room, where he shows you a wonderful suit of golden armour with a hawk's-head breast plate, for you to wear. He also gives you a leather pouch with 10 Gold Pieces in it. Finally he offers you a magnificent sword, made of the finest steel. As you draw it from its scabbard, you are taken aback when the sword suddenly speaks to you.

`Let's get something straight. I'm not going to chop up any old monster. You've got to get my permission first, or I may decide not to fight. All right?' The sword speaks in a sharp, high-pitched voice.

`Oh, just ignore the sword,' Marris says reassuringly. `Although he's got a grumpy side, he's still the finest sword in the land. And he actually has a name: it's Edge. Now, you must set off on your quest for the crown without further delay. The sooner the people believe that Prince Goldhawk is alive and well, the better. Nobody else knows our secret. Orlando will go with you to show you the way. Good luck, my friend.'

Soon you find yourself walking out through the castle gates with Orlando at your side to start your magical quest.

Now go to the next page and make a note that your fighting SKILL is 8 and that you have 10 Gold Pieces. Keep a record of your gold and other items you find during your adventure. If your fighting SKILL is reduced to zero, you will have died and must start again.

1

You set off eastwards on foot, and Karazan Castle is soon left far behind. It is a warm autumn day and you are amazed at the beauty of the land through which you are walking.

`Can't you walk a little slower?' Orlando squeals, scampering along on his little trotters.

`If you were wise, like me,' Edge says proudly, `you would get someone to carry you.'

`That's only because you haven't got any legs,' Orlando replies snappily.

`Now listen, you two,' you interrupt, `that's enough of that. We've only just set off, and already you are arguing!'

You continue for another hour until you come to a fast-flowing river.

`Don't expect me to swim across,' Orlando says nervously. `There's a bridge, not far upstream, where we can cross.'

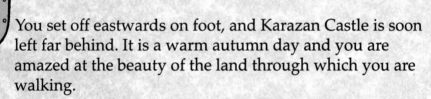

When you get there, it is guarded by a frightening-looking man dressed from head to toe in spiked, black armour. In his right hand he is holding a heavy morning star which he swings menacingly from side to side.

`Before you can cross my bridge, you will have to pay me five Gold Pieces!' he bawls out in a threatening voice.

If you are willing to pay 5 Gold Pieces to cross the bridge, go to **1A**. If you prefer to fight the Dark Knight, go to **1B**.

1A   The Knight snatches the gold from you before moving to one side to let you pass.

`If you ask me,' whispers Edge, `I think we could have done him in.'

`Let's just get on with our search,' you reply. `We won't miss a few Gold Pieces.' Go to **1E**.

1B   `Do I have your permission, Edge?' you ask your sword, tongue in cheek.

`You most certainly have!' comes the reply at once.

The Dark Knight grunts and starts to swing his morning star weapon above his head.

Fighting is worked out by means of dice rolls. The Dark Knight has a SKILL of 7. You have a SKILL of 8, and you attack first. Roll two dice. If the total of the two dice is 7 or higher, you slay the Dark Knight. Go to 1C. If the total rolled is less than 7, he blocks your blow. Roll both dice again, this time for the Dark Knight's attack upon you. If the total is 8 or higher, his blow strikes you. Go to 1D. If neither you nor the Dark Knight lands a blow, roll the dice again until you or the Dark Knight wins.

1C You step over the body of the Dark Knight and cross the bridge. Go to **1E**.

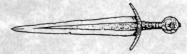

1D You stagger back from the weight of the blow. The Dark Knight strides towards you, still swinging his morning star. Just as he is about to strike again, Orlando curls up into a ball and rolls into him at full speed, knocking him on to his back. The Knight's armour is so heavy that he can't get back on to his feet again. But you are wounded yourself: from now on, your SKILL is 7. You walk slowly across the bridge. Go to **1E**.

1E After some time, the path you are walking along divides in two and one fork leads south towards the hills. Pointing east on an old wooden signpost is `Longshadow Forest' and to the south, `Vanish'. While you are making up your mind which way to go, a large black crow swoops down and settles on the rickety signpost.

`Mister Prince!' the crow squawks. `Marris has sent me to tell you that you must wear the Golden Hand wristlet when you come to tackle Darkmoon. It is hidden in the Howling Tunnels.'

The crow flies off, but nobody has any idea where the Howling Tunnels are. If you want to go to the Longshadow Forest, go to **5**. If you want to go to Vanish, go to **15**.

2 You trudge slowly through the forest and have almost reached the far edge when the sound of somebody chopping wood comes to your ears. You walk in the direction of the noise, and soon you discover a huge, bald-headed man wielding a two-handed axe – not at a tree, but at a Treeman. The Treeman groans in a deep voice as a chunk of wood is sliced from his trunk and he tries to club the Axeman with his branches.

'Help me, stranger!' the Axeman cries. 'Cut through the vine that is gripping my leg before it's too late.'

'This evil man is trying to kill me for my magic sap,' the Treeman says in a deep voice, full of pain. 'It is me you should help.' If you want to save the Axeman, go to **2A**. If you prefer to disarm the Axeman, go to **2B**.

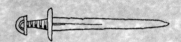

2A With one swipe of your sword, you cut through the vine holding the Axeman's leg. He reels back, then he starts to laugh.

'What a fool you are,' he says with a sneer. 'Now I'll be taking your fancy gold armour if you don't mind. Or I can put some serious dents in it, if you wish to leave it on!'

'You will pay for your evil,' you shout as you step forward and into battle.

Fighting is worked out by means of dice rolls. The Axeman has a SKILL *of 7. You attack first and you have a* SKILL *of 8 if this is your first battle. Roll two dice. If the total of the two dice is 7 or higher, you slay the Axeman. Go to* **2C**. *If the total rolled is 6 or less, the Axeman manages to block your blow. Roll both dice again, this time for the Axeman. If the total is the same as, or higher than, your* SKILL, *his blow strikes you. Go to* **2D**. *If neither you nor the Axeman lands a blow, roll the dice again, taking turns, until one of you hits the other.*

2B You grab hold of the axe and this allows the Treeman to tighten his grip on the Axeman, who curses you loudly.

'Darkmoon will make you pay for this!' the Axeman shouts.
Go to **2C**.

2C `Prince Goldhawk will always help good defeat evil,' Orlando says proudly.

`You are the Prince of Karazan?' the Treeman asks softly. `In that case I shall be honoured if Prince Goldhawk will add a few drops of my magic sap to his water-bottle.' Trusting the gentle Treeman, you do as he asks and then you drink the water. Add 1 to your SKILL.

`Now you must find Lady Helena,' the Treeman continues. `She will tell you the way to the Howling Tunnels. She lives in Westwater or Eastwater – I can't remember which. It's my memory, you know.'

You thank the Treeman for his advice and walk out of the forest. If you wish to set off to the west, go to **13**. If you prefer to head east, go to **19**.

2D You are wounded in the leg, but not seriously. Lose 1 SKILL point. Luckily, Orlando comes to your rescue. He charges into the Axeman and sends him flying back into the grip of the Treeman again. Go to **2B**.

3 The tunnel is narrow and has a low ceiling. You walk on, but you have the clear feeling that you are being watched.

`If I had any hairs on my neck, they would be standing on end,' Orlando whispers, for he too is aware of the unseen eyes.

At last the tunnel opens out into a small cavern. In the middle, a great bubbling cauldron is hanging over a crackling fire. There are lots of wooden cages of various sizes in the cavern: small ones hang from the ceiling, while

others stand on the floor, but they all have an animal of some sort inside them. Suddenly, from out of every nook and cranny in the cavern appear several short reddish brown-skinned creatures. They have long noses and ears and they wear a menacing look on their small faces. Each is armed with a short bow which is pointing straight at you.

`Oh no, Troglodytes!' Orlando shrieks. `If we don't give them some gems, we'll end up in that pot.'

If you have some gems, go to **3A**. If you do not have any gems, go to **3B**.

3A You slowly take the sparkling gems out of your pouch. The Troglodytes mutter excitedly.

`I'm going to throw the gems in the air and let those creatures fight over them. Get ready to run, Orlando,' you say in a low voice.

As soon as the gems land on the floor, the Troglodytes pile on top of one another, screeching loudly. You turn and run, not stopping to look behind you. You run back along the tunnel and into the other one. Go to **9**.

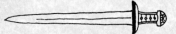

3B `We could make a run for it,' Orlando suggests.

`Or we could fight,' Edge adds.

`Either way you lose!' a squeaky voice behind you says.

A heavy net suddenly drops down from above, trapping you underneath. The tiny creatures cluster around, prodding you with sticks and taking everything you have. Later, you are put in a wooden cage until it is your turn in the cauldron.

You have failed in your quest and your adventure is over.

4

The corridor ends at another flight of steps. You climb these until you reach another trapdoor. You push it up and find that it opens on to the outside world. There is a chill in the air and Orlando complains of being cold and hungry.

`We may stop at the next village for some food, as long as the villagers are friendly,' you say, cheering him up. `But we must press on with our quest and find the Crown of Karazan.'

An hour later you notice a strange creature coming towards you; it looks like a giant beetle and every so often it stops, raises its front legs and squirts a jet of white liquid on to the ground.

`What in the world is that?' you ask.

`It's a Litterbug,' Orlando replies. `They are a real nuisance: they make a mess all over the countryside, and they are poisonous, too.'

Suddenly you hear the sound of galloping hoofs thundering across the plain. A Centaur, half man and half horse, gallops up to the Litterbug and attacks it with a long spear. The Litterbug raises its front legs again and tries to spray the Centaur with its poison, but the Centaur is too quick for it. It circles the Litterbug, jabbing at it with the spear until the Litterbug falls at last. The Centaur rears up and waves its spear in triumph. If you wish to talk to the Centaur, go to **4A**. If you would rather walk on, go to **4B**.

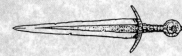

4A   The Centaur is an ally of Karazan and is willing to help you in your quest, although it does not know where the Howling Tunnels are to be found.

`I'll take you to the village where the Big Blue Mice live. They may sound a little odd, but they know everything. If

you offer them a gift, they will tell you where to find the tunnels for sure.'

You climb on to the Centaur's back and, holding Orlando safely in front of you, you gallop off across the plain at a wild speed. When a village comes into view, the Centaur bids you good luck and farewell. Go to **7**.

4B You trudge on across the plain without anything interesting happening, until suddenly you hear a loud buzzing sound in the sky. A swarm of Killer Bees swoops down and attacks you. You are stung over and over again, but you survive. You do lose 2 SKILL points, however. Orlando fares much better, as he is defended by his iron-like skin. You walk on, feeling very uncomfortable, but at last a village comes into view. Go to **7**.

An eerie-looking forest soon comes into view. The trees are dense and have crooked roots, making it difficult to walk.

`This is no place for a picnic,' Orlando whispers. `But look, over there is a clearing.'

You walk towards the place where he is pointing. Here you see a small thin man sitting on a very large mushroom with his arms crossed. He is humming a song and seems quite unaware of anything. When you get near, though, he opens one eye and scowls at you. When Orlando sneezes suddenly, the colourful bird that was sitting on the Gnome's shoulder flies up into the trees.

`Now look what you've done, you fools!' the Gnome shouts. `Is it any wonder that I live in this forest, to get away from clumsy idiots like you! Before I turn you both into frogs,

would you care to tell me what you are doing here?'

If you wish to tell the Gnome about your quest, go to **5A**. If you would rather attack the Gnome, go to **5B**.

5A `Hey, hey, hey, this is your lucky day!' the Gnome says excitedly as he jumps off the mushroom to shake your hand. `My name is Finzy Fecklegum, I'm a wizard by trade and a hermit by nature. I am very pleased to meet you, but I do wish you hadn't scared away my pet Firebird. If the Orcs capture it, they'll eat it and use its feathers for a head-dress. And there are plenty of Orcs in the forest. Find my bird before the Orcs do, and fortune will smile on you.'

If you want to search for the Firebird, go to **10**. If you would rather continue your search for the Howling Tunnels, go to **2**.

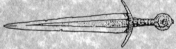

5B `I don't think this is a good idea,' Edge says quickly. `What good will come from attacking a Gnome? Besides, he must be able to defend himself if he lives in this dismal forest.' If you are determined to attack the Gnome, go to **5C**. If you prefer to change your mind and tell him about your quest, go to **5A**.

5C `Boring, boring, boring,' the Gnome says calmly as you draw your sword. He reaches into his pocket, pulls out a handful of sparkling dust and throws it over you. In seconds you are transformed into a frog and you hop off into the forest with a croak. You have failed in your quest and your adventure ends.

You run as fast as you can, with Orlando huffing and puffing beside you and the guards not far behind.

`There's a hole at the foot of that wall just ahead,' Orlando gasps. `I'm sure you'll manage to squeeze through. Follow me!'

Orlando runs into the hole and out the other side without even having to slow down. You dive through after him in a cloud of dust. Then you quickly block the hole off with a boulder which you roll into place. You find yourself outside the town walls. Night is approaching, but you decide it is safer to be out in the open than inside Eastwater. The light quickly fades as you walk across the plain outside the town.

`Where are we going to sleep?' Orlando asks.

You look around and in the distance you spot a stone house. As you come closer to it, you see that its walls are broken and it has no roof. By the time you reach it, a full moon is riding high above in the night sky. All is eerily still – until a wolf's howl breaks the silence.

`Maybe we should have stayed in Eastwater after all,' Orlando whispers. You enter the ruined house and find a room with a broken bed in it. You make yourself comfortable by covering it with some old straw.

You talk with Orlando and Edge far into the night about the mystery and dangers of Karazan, until you fall asleep.

Some time later, you are woken by the sound of footsteps outside the house. A dark shape suddenly appears in the doorway, its face hidden by a black cape. Then suddenly you see its white face with red eyes and two long fangs protruding from its upper jaw. A Vampire! You leap up, shouting an alarm to Orlando.

If you wish to use your sword to fight the Vampire, go to

6A. If you have some garlic to use against the Vampire, go
to **6B**.

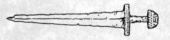

6A   The Vampire is not afraid of Edge, who cannot wound
this undead creature of the night. The monster steps
forward to wrap its cape round you and sinks its fangs
into you. You have failed in your quest and your
adventure is over.

6B If you hold the garlic in front of you, the Vampire will be halted in its tracks. It cowers back and goes out through the door to escape the pungent fumes of the garlic. You see a trapdoor in the middle of the floor and pull its handle. The trapdoor rises and reveals a flight of stone steps that lead down into the gloom. Orlando scampers down the steps without being told, and you follow quickly after him, torch in hand, bolting the trapdoor behind you. Go to **18**.

7 Making straight for the village, you are surprised to see that all the houses are painted blue. You also see that all the inhabitants are blue mice, and big mice at that, standing on their hind legs as tall as any human.

'These mice don't look very dangerous,' you say with some relief. 'Let's ask them if they know where the Howling Tunnels are, Orlando.'

You walk over to a smithy, where a Big Blue Mouse is hard at work beating a sword into shape on an anvil.

`Good morning, my name is Prince Goldhawk of Karazan and this is my servant, Orlando,' you say boldly. `Could you please tell me where I will find the Howling Tunnels. The fate of my kingdom rests on it.'

`Fi uoy evig em emos fo ym etiruovaf eulb eseehc, I lliw llet uoy woh ot teg ereht,' the Big Blue Mouse says in a high-pitched voice.

If you understand what the mouse wants, go to **7A**. If you do not understand what he wants, go to **7C**.

7A If you have some blue cheese to give to the Blue Mouse, go to **7B**. If you do not have any blue cheese, go to **7C**.

7B The Big Blue Mouse squeaks with excitement when you give it the cheese, and it starts nibbling at it straight away. When it has eaten enough, it starts to speak again.

`Suoiciled!' the mouse squeaks. `Won netsil ylluferac. Eht Gnilwoh Slennut era yrev suoregnad. Eraweb eht Taerg Erif Nogard. Og htron morf ereh litnu uoy ees eht etihw kcor. Uoy lliw dnif eht ecnartne ereht.'

You thank the mouse for this information and leave the village to head north. Go to **11**.

7C You leave the village and walk on across the plain, until finally you arrive at a wooded hillside and find some fruit to eat.

`I recognize these woods,' Orlando suddenly says with a start. `Maggot Manor lies inside them, oh yes, oh yes!'

`Well, wristlet or not, let's pay Darkmoon a visit!' you answer cheerfully. Go to **16**.

8

You keep walking along the dungeon corridor for some time, until at last you come to a heavy iron door in the left-hand wall. You open the door, and there sits a hideous brown-skinned creature, chained to the left wall by one leg.

`A Bonecrusher!' Orlando says, and he sounds sure he is right.

A wooden chest stands against the right-hand wall, and a lantern is burning on top of it, but you are not at all sure whether the chained beast can reach it.

`I wonder what is in that chest,' Orlando mutters.

If you want to go in and try to pick up the chest, go to **8A**. If you would rather close the door and walk on along the corridor, go to **4**.

8A As you enter the room, the Bonecrusher lets out a mighty roar and moves slowly towards you with its clawed hands out-stretched. If you have drunk a Potion of Good Fortune, go to **8B**. If you have not drunk this potion, go to **8C**.

8B You are very lucky indeed. The chain stops the Bonecrusher from reaching the chest. Go to **8E**.

8C You are unlucky. The Bonecrusher's chain is long enough for it to guard the chest. If you want to fight the Bonecrusher, go to **8D**. If you would rather leave the room and walk on along the corridor, go to **4**.

8D The Bonecrusher is a fierce fighter and its strength is very great. But you and Edge the sword are ready for combat.

Fighting is worked out by means of dice rolls. The Bonecrusher has a SKILL of 9. You should have made a note of your present SKILL, which started at 8. You attack first. Roll two dice. If the total of the two dice is 9 or higher, you win against the Bonecrusher. Go to 8E. If the total rolled is 8 or less, the Bonecrusher blocks your blow. Roll both dice again, this time for the Bonecrusher's attack. If the total is the same as, or higher than, your present SKILL, its blow is fatal – you have failed in your quest and your adventure is over. If neither you nor the Bonecrusher lands a blow, roll the dice again, taking turns, until one of you hits the other.

8E You open the chest, and inside it you find an old map. In dark curving script you read the words 'Howling Tunnels' above a diagram of passages inside a cave. The map also says: 'Beware the Troglodytes of the Sun Cavern'. You fold the map away and walk along the corridor. Go to **4**.

As you walk along the tunnel, the screaming grows louder and begins to sound more like a chilling howl.

'We must be near our goal,' you say reassuringly.

You come to the way into another cavern, and your eyes widen with glee when you notice a marble fountain inside. The fountain is shaped like a young nymph, and water gently trickles out of the urn she is holding. But it is the golden wristlet on her left arm that interests you most: it is in the shape of a hand! But your joy does not last long when a wailing old woman jumps out from behind the statue.

'Sword help us!' Orlando exclaims. 'It's a Banshee!'

Clearly, Orlando is very upset by the howling Banshee, and he is trembling with fear. You will have to fight this deadly opponent alone.

Fighting is worked out by means of dice rolls. The Banshee has a SKILL of 9 because its fear-inducing howl makes it even stronger. You should have made a note of your present SKILL, which started at 8. You attack first. Roll two dice. If the total of the two dice is 9 or higher, you slay the Banshee. Go to 9A. If the total rolled is 8 or less, the Banshee blocks your attack. Roll both dice again, this time for the Banshee. If the total is the same as, or higher than, your SKILL, you are hit. Go to 9B. If neither you nor the Banshee lands a blow, roll the dice again until either you or the Banshee lands a blow.

9A You step over the Banshee and wade across the fountain to get the wristlet. You pull it carefully off the nymph's arm and look at it closely, marvelling at how well it has been made. If you want to put it on your right wrist, go to 9C. If you want to put it on your left wrist, go to 9D.

9B The Banshee lets out another blood-curdling howl as you clutch at the gash on your cheek. You, too, become transfixed with fear and now are easy prey for the Banshee to finish off.

You have failed in your quest and your adventure is over.

9C You are just admiring the golden wristlet when suddenly you feel full of energy and courage. Its magical powers add 2 to your SKILL. You search through the cave until you find a secret door which opens on to the bare hillside. You breathe in the fresh air, happy to be outside again. Now Orlando is keen to prove his worth and he leads you to the wooded hillside where Maggot Manor lies. Go to **16**.

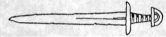

9D You are just admiring the golden wristlet when suddenly all your skin begins to tighten and a terrible pain spreads through your bones. Slowly your whole body stiffens, and you turn into marble, as did the nymph.

 You have failed in your quest and your adventure is over.

 You walk further and further into the forest, cutting your way through with your sword, which complains bitterly at having to carry out such a boring task. An hour has passed when Orlando suddenly stops to sniff the air.

'Orcs!' he whispers. 'They can't be far away. I can smell their stinkyness, oh yes, oh yes.'

You quietly step through the long grass as far as the edge of another clearing, and here you see two ugly green-skinned Orcs. One of them is firing arrows into the upper

branches of the trees, while the other one is pointing and shouting loudly in Orcish.

`What are they shouting about?' you ask.

`It's the Firebird,' Orlando replies. `It's too exhausted to fly on and it's trying to hide in one of those trees. It changes the colour of its feathers so it can blend in with its background, but the Orcs have spotted it.'

`Let's get them,' Edge says quickly. `I'm tired of being used to hack through vines.'

`Orlando, you bowl over the archer while Edge and I take care of the other one,' you say quietly. `Right, let's go!'

*Fighting is worked out by means of dice rolls. The Orc has a SKILL of 6. You attack first, and you have a SKILL of 8 if this is your first battle. Roll two dice. If the total of the two dice is 6 or higher, you slay the Orc. Go to **10A**. If the total rolled is 5 or* *less, the Orc manages to stop your blow. Roll both dice again, this time for the Orc's attack against you. If the total is the same as, or higher than, your* SKILL, *its blow strikes you. Go to* **10B**. *If neither you nor the Orc lands a blow, roll the dice again, taking it in turns, until one of you hits the other.*

10A You turn to see how Orlando is getting on. He did manage to knock the Orc down, but now it is getting slowly to its feet again, sword in hand. It's still slightly dazed, so you creep up behind it to thump it on the head with a branch.

Look at the picture opposite. The Firebird is hidden somewhere on the page. If you find it, you will see what colour it is. If you think it is red, go to **10C**. If you think it is blue, go to **10D**. If you think it is green, go to **10E**.

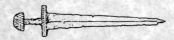

10B You stagger back from the blow. The Orc closes in for the kill, but suddenly your sword starts slashing through the air all by itself, and it makes quick work of the Orc, which can hardly believe its eyes. Your wound has made you weaker, however. Reduce your SKILL by 1. Go to **10A**.

10C The Firebird does not have red feathers. You do not spot it before it flies off again. Now you have no choice but to continue your quest. Go to **2**.

10D The Firebird does not have blue feathers. You do not spot it before it flies off again. Now you have no choice but to continue your quest. Go to **2**.

10E The Firebird does have green feathers. You climb up the trunk of the tree and bring the bird down carefully. Then you walk back to Finzy Fecklegum, who is overjoyed to get his Firebird back. Before you set off again, he gives you a Ring of Lightning as his way of saying `Thank you'. Go to **2**.

By midday the ground has become rocky and bare, and you start climbing towards some mountains. An hour later, you spot a great white rock concealing the entrance to a cave.

`At last we have reached the Howling Tunnels,' you say with a sigh. `Come on, Orlando, let's get on with it.'

You enter the cave. It is cold and dank but is lit by burning torches that have been set in the wall. Some way into the cave, you see the shape of a large figure, leaning against the wall. It does not move as you approach and soon you see why: it is a large Cave Troll guard. It is sound asleep and is snoring loudly. Its ugly green face is covered in warts, and long yellow teeth stick out of its fat jaws at odd angles. If you have drunk a Potion of Good Fortune, go to **11A**. If you have not drunk this potion, go to **11B**.

11A You leave the Cave Troll behind and walk on down the tunnel.

`What's that noise?' Orlando asks suddenly. `It sounds a bit like a muffled scream.'

`Probably a Tin Pig, looking in the mirror,' Edge jokes.

`Come on, let's keep going,' you say quickly. Go to **14**.

11B Orlando feels a tickle inside his nose and he cannot stop himself sneezing. The Cave Troll jumps up and gets wild when he sees strangers in front of him. He picks up his spiked club and grunts loudly.

Fighting is worked out by means of dice rolls. The Cave Troll has a SKILL of 7. You should have kept a record of your present SKILL, which started at 8. You attack first. Roll two dice. If the total of the two dice is 7 or higher, you slay the Cave Troll. Go to 11A. If the total rolled is 6 or less, the Cave Troll blocks your blow. Roll both dice again, this time for the Cave Troll. If the total is the same as, or higher than, your SKILL, his club hits you. Go to 11C. If neither you nor the Cave Troll lands a blow, roll the dice again, taking turns, until one of you hits the other.

11C You are knocked to the ground by the heavy blow. Lose 1 SKILL point. Orlando comes to your rescue, however, bowling the Troll over with one of his famous rolling attacks. The Cave Troll hits his head on a rock and is knocked unconscious. Go to **11A**.

12 It is not long before you find yourself walking past the dirty window of a small shop. It is crammed full of weird and wonderful things: strange weapons, jars of teeth, dusty old books, clay pots, carpets with odd patterns on them and other stuff are piled high and they look as if they haven't been touched in

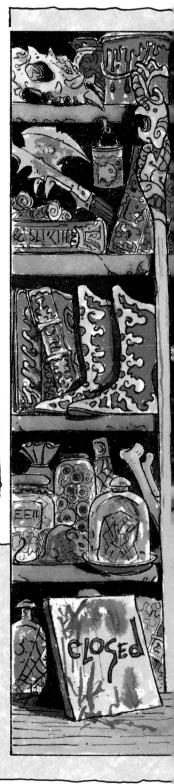

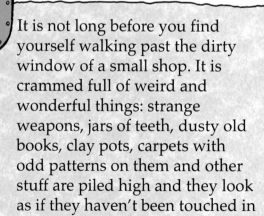

years. You decide to enter the shop, even though the sign says `Closed'.

A bell rings as you open the door and a man with not much hair and a shiny forehead that stretches right over the top of his head pops up from behind the counter. He wears a frown that never seems to leave his face.

`Can't you read?' he says in a gruff voice. `Have you got a head of lead or is my name not Domehead? This shop is closed – and nothing is for sale anyway.'

If you want to ask Domehead if he would like to swap something, go to **12A**. If you want to ask him about the Howling Tunnels, go to **12D**.

12A `Now you're talking!' Domehead says excitedly. `I love swapping. What have you got to trade?'

If you have a Potion of Invisibility that you would like to trade, go to **12B**. If you have a Ring of Ice that you wish to trade, go to **12C**.

12B Domehead rubs his chin, then he says, `For that I'll offer you a Magic Arrow, a mirror and a Dragon's tooth.' If you want to swap the potion for these goods, make a note of them. Go to **12E**.

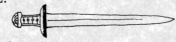

12C Domehead rubs his chin, then he says, `For that I'll offer you a pair of Elven Boots, a Magic Staff and some Blue Cheese.' If you want to swap the ring for these things, make a note of them. Go to **12E**.

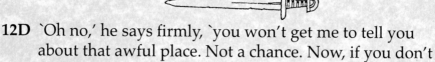

12D `Oh no,' he says firmly, `you won't get me to tell you about that awful place. Not a chance. Now, if you don't mind, I've got things to do. Goodbye.'

Domehead disappears into a back room and he won't come back out again. Go to **12E**.

12E `Well, Orlando, I guess that's that. We'd better be on our way,' you say.

No sooner are you out of the shop than Domehead appears at the door and starts shouting, `Thief! Thief! Stop that thief!' at the top of his voice. Four heavily armed guards come running, and you decide to make a run for it too, as you are unlikely to get any justice in a town that is full of rogues, as Eastwater seems to be. You dash along an alley until you come to a turning. If you want to turn to the left, go to **17**. If you want to turn to the right, go to **6**.

Glad to be out of the forest at last, you walk with a spring in your step, much to the annoyance of Orlando, who has difficulty keeping up. Travelling westwards, you come to a valley. In it is a village, above which hangs a soft, purple haze sparkling in the sunshine.

`Westwater, I presume,' Orlando says cheerfully.

You enter the village and are immediately surrounded by cheering Elves who recognize you as the Prince.

`They wouldn't be so happy if they knew I was a Dwarf,' Orlando whispers, reminding you that the two races dislike each other, even though both fought on the side of good.

The Elves invite you to meet their leader, and you follow them to a nearby glade where the purple haze surrounds a lemon tree. Sitting on an ornate wooden throne and reading a book is a beautiful young woman. She has a wonderfully happy smile, and you suddenly realize that all the lemons on the tree are smiling too. It is a quite extraordinary sight.

`Welcome, Prince. I am Lady Helena,' the woman says, nodding her head. `I understand that you come seeking my help. Darkmoon and his Orcs are our enemy, too. Ask, and I will do what I can.'

You tell Lady Helena that you are searching for the Golden Hand wristlet, which you have been told is hidden in the Howling Tunnels.

`The Golden Hand!' she exclaims. `That is a very strong magical article. It was stolen from us Elves many years ago. It would be useless for you to try to use it without knowing its secret. Be sure to wear it on your right wrist. Remember that. I am sure that you will also need some more protection for your journey. Here, take this garlic which will guard you against the undead. And drink this

Potion of Good Fortune to bring you good luck. Follow your heart and you will win over the evil that threatens us all. But first you must go to a place of evil yourself. I am unable to name that place, but if you count the lemons on my tree you will know where to go. Farewell, my Prince.'

Count the lemons on the tree and go to the section with that number, taking with you fond memories of the beautiful Lady Helena.

14

Again you hear the muffled scream coming from the tunnel ahead of you. It is definitely a woman's scream. Then you hear footsteps running away and the sound of a hysterical laugh.

`Who *is* that?' Orlando asks in a whisper.

`I'm sure we'll soon find out,' you reply.

The tunnels are quiet again and you walk on, trying not to make any noise yourself. You can see a red glow in the distance and you hear a roar like the sound of a big fire. You tip-toe as far as the entrance to a huge cave, and there is an enormous red-scaled Dragon, asleep, with flames coming from its mouth. Its long tail flicks slowly from side to side, rolling old bones noisily across the stone floor. There is another tunnel in the far wall of the cave.

`It's a Great Fire Dragon,' Orlando whispers. `I knew they existed, but I never dreamed I would ever see one. It's so big! It must be very old. How are we going to get past it?'

If you have a Potion of Invisibility, go to **14A**. If you do not have this potion, go to **14B**.

14A 'It's a good job we kept Sad Sam's potion and didn't let that swindler Domehead have it,' you say quietly as you share the potion with Orlando.

'Where have you gone, Prince Goldhawk?' Orlando asks worriedly.

'I'm here,' you reply softly. 'We're both invisible! I can't see you either. Now walk round, past the Dragon, and I'll meet you in the tunnel opposite. Let's hurry. The potion could wear off at any moment.'

You walk round the slumbering Dragon as quickly as possible and then you enter the new tunnel. By the time you reach the place where the tunnel splits, you are both completely visible again. Carved into the wall of the tunnel to your left there is the sign of a crescent moon. In the tunnel to your right there is the sign of a sun. This tunnel is deadly quiet but again you can hear the same woman's scream coming from the left-hand tunnel, only now it is louder. If you want to enter the tunnel where the screaming is coming from, go to **9**. If you want to enter the right-hand tunnel, go to **3**.

14B 'Let's try to sneak round behind the Dragon. Perhaps it's too sleepy to notice us,' you whisper.

'If you say so,' Orlando replies in a trembling voice.

You press yourself against the wall of the cavern and get halfway, when the great beast suddenly cranes its neck around. Its small sparkling eyes catch sight of you and you feel like a trapped animal.

'Run, Orlando, run for your life!' you shout. But it is too late. One blast of its fiery breath is enough to prepare its dinner.

You have failed in your quest and your adventure is over.

The path wanders through the hills and comes at last to a village. Crossing a stone bridge, you see a sign marked `Vanish'. As you enter the village you notice that all the people living here look thoroughly miserable and grumpy. Some are frowning, others are scowling, some are sneering, but no one is laughing.

`What a funny name for a village,' Orlando says. `Why don't you have a word with one of them, Goldhawk, and ask them how they came by it?'

You walk over to a lanky fellow dressed in baggy clothes, and he introduces himself as Sad Sam. He explains that they are all miserable because they keep losing everything they own. It's been going on for years, he says. They can't understand it, but holes keep appearing in pockets, bags rip open, purses are dropped and everything just keeps disappearing. It has happened so often that now the villagers are beginning to suspect one another.

`Take today, for example. I have already lost three items myself: a key with the number of my house on it, a clay bottle with a Potion of Invisibility in it, and a gold ring that just slipped off my finger. It's a magical ring too, a Ring of Ice. For the life of me, I can't find it. I bet old Grumpy Greta has got them – the way she follows me around all day as though she's got nothing better to do. Mind you, she's lost a few things herself. If you give me four Gold Pieces, you can have them all – if you can find them!'

If you fancy giving Sad Sam 4 Gold Pieces to look for his lost possessions, go to **15A**. Otherwise, to leave this depressing place and walk back to Longshadow Forest; go to **5**.

15A Sad Sam has to think long and hard about where to put the Gold Pieces. Finally he finds a shirt pocket without any holes in it and drops the coins into it before he walks slowly away, muttering to himself. You begin your search of the village. If you find any of the three items, make a note of the number on the key, the colour of the clay bottle and the letter on the ring. When you finish your search, you leave Vanish and head for Longshadow Forest. Go to **5**.

16

Following Orlando, you soon arrive outside Maggot Manor. It is a forbidding place with high walls and tall, dark towers.

`I know the way in, but you will have to carry me, Goldhawk,' Orlando says apologetically. `Swimming and climbing no longer come easily to me!' With Orlando under one arm, you swim across the moat and climb the walls. Putting him down before you cross the courtyard, you suddenly spot a Lizard Man guard appearing through an archway, although he does not see you.

If you are wearing Elven Boots, go to **16A**. If you are not wearing these boots, go to **16B**.

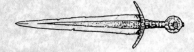

16A You pick Orlando up again and run across the courtyard in a blur of speed without the Lizard Man noticing you. Then you hide behind a wall, and your boots are still smoking from covering the ground so fast.

`Better slow down a bit, Goldhawk,' Orlando suggests. `We can walk from now on. You can put me down.'

`I'll put you down!' jokes Edge.

You follow Orlando through the maze until at last you reach Darkmoon's much-feared herb garden. Orlando trots over to the tree where he was trapped only two days ago.

`Not this time,' he says cheerfully.

`Let's go inside,' you decide, turning the handle of the door that leads to Darkmoon's private rooms. Go to **20**.

16B The Lizard Man turns and sees you. Before he can raise the alarm, you attack him with the sword.

*Fighting is worked out by means of dice rolls. The Lizard Man has a SKILL of 9. You should have kept a record of your present SKILL, which started at 8. You attack first. Roll two dice. If the total of the two dice is 9 or higher, you defeat the Lizard Man. Go to **16C**. If the total rolled is 8 or less, the Lizard Man avoids your blow. Roll both dice again, this time for the Lizard Man. If the total is the same as, or higher than, your present SKILL, his spear-thrust is fatal: you have failed in your quest and your adventure is over. If neither you nor the Lizard Man lands a blow, roll the dice again until one of you hits the other.*

16C After hurrying across the courtyard, you follow Orlando through the maze and finally reach Darkmoon's herb garden. Orlando trots over to the tree up which he was trapped only two days ago.

'Not this time,' he says cheerfully.

'Let's go inside,' you say firmly, turning the handle of the door that leads to Darkmoon's private chambers. Go to **20**.

17

The alley comes to a dead end. The walls here are too high to climb: there is no escape. You turn to face the guards, who are marching towards you in a line with their pikes pointing at you.

`Stand where you are, thief, and surrender,' one of the guards yells out.

`Let's get them!' Edge suddenly pipes up, and you are quick to agree. You run towards the guards and are just about to strike the one who spoke when you feel a stinging pain in your neck. You have been hit by a poisoned dart, fired by one of the other guards. You stagger forward, then fall to the ground, unconscious. When you wake up, you find yourself locked in a dingy cell with Orlando.

`How are you feeling, Prince Goldhawk?' Orlando asks you with some concern.

`I feel terrible,' you reply, feeling rotten. `Where's my sword?'

`I'm over here!' Edge calls out grumpily.

Through the bars you can see Edge, hanging over the back of a chair. There are no guards to be seen.

`How are we going to escape?' Orlando asks. `Much as I would like to, I'm afraid I cannot leap off this chair, hop over to your cell and cut through the bars,' Edge says snootily. `You'll just have to think of something for yourselves.'

`If only we had a key,' Orlando says hopefully. As your head clears, it dawns on you that you may have a key. If you have, go to **17A**. If you do not have a key, go to **17B**.

17A If you have a key, you will be able to open the cell door with it, collect your sword and escape. The only key that will open the door has a number engraved on it. If you

know the number, go to the section with the same number. If you do not know the number, go to **17B**.

17B The hours pass slowly until at last a guard appears with a bowl of lukewarm porridge for you to eat.

`Don't worry!' the guard laughs. `You'll be out of here in two years!'

You have failed in your quest, and your adventure is over.

At the bottom of the steps, a corridor leads away, into the distance. There are pools of foul liquid on the floor and you hear a steady dripping of water echoing around you. The air has an old, musty smell and the walls are wet with slime. A rat scurries past and vanishes. You walk along the corridor, and soon you come to a heavy wooden door with `Keep Out' written on it in red. You press your ear to the door and you can hear scratching sounds coming from the other side.

`Might as well go in,' you say cheerfully as Orlando looks doubtfully at the door.

You turn the handle and enter a square, stone-walled room, the floor of which is covered with large, black, hairy-legged spiders. A rope is hanging down from the middle of the ceiling and on the end of it you can see a leather pouch. There is a wooden door in the far wall. Orlando walks ahead of you and for a moment you think he's just going to walk straight in. Then suddenly he stops.

`After you, sire,' Orlando says jokingly.

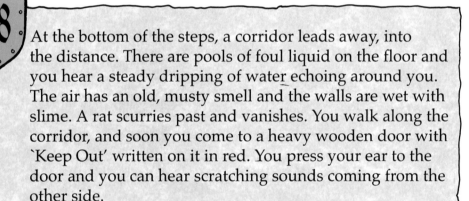

If you want to run through the spiders to get the pouch, go to **18A**. If you would rather shut the door again and walk down the corridor, go to **8**.

18A The spiders are harmless and not at all poisonous. Orlando follows you into the room. As soon as you take the pouch, however, the door behind you slams shut. You hear a grinding, grating noise – then you realize that the walls on either side are closing in on you! If you have a magic staff, you may wish to use it here. If so, go to **18B**. If you do not have a staff, you could try opening the door opposite. Go to **18C**.

18B Standing in the middle of the room with your staff stretched out in front of you, you watch as the rumbling walls keep closing in.

`Cross your fingers!' you say out loud.

`Fingers? We haven't got any fingers to cross!' Edge and Orlando both say at the same time. The walls close in until they are touching the ends of the staff. It starts to creak and bend under the pressure, but then it suddenly straightens out again: the walls have been stopped in their tracks. Orlando gives out a cheer. Inside the pouch you find three gems: a diamond, a ruby and an emerald. The door in the far wall is locked, but you find that the door you came in by has opened again. You decide to leave the spider room and continue along the corridor. Go to **8**.

18C The door is locked and there is no escape. The walls keep closing in until at last they squash you.

Your search has failed and your adventure is over.

At the foot of the hills you come to a village which is almost hidden by shadows. A weather-beaten sign reads `Eastwater – strangers not welcome', but you decide to go on. Entering the village, you can sense at once that the people living here are scared of something. A few people hurry past, and no one stops to speak to you. A bell tolls, its deep chime sending a shiver down your back. From an open upstairs window you hear a worried voice cry out:

`It is the hour when the beast feasts! Lock your doors! The beast feasts!' And all at once the streets are deserted, with not a soul in sight. A frightening roar breaks the silence and you draw your sword.

`I think that down that alley on the left there is something we don't want to meet,' Orlando whispers nervously. You walk boldly to the end of the alley and meet a hideous monster wearing a battered chainmail coat. It has a skull head with a terrifying long jaw from which a steady stream of foul liquid drips.

`The Skullbeast!' Orlando whispers. `I hope it hates the taste of Tin Pigs!'

`We'll protect you, don't you worry,' Edge says, just to tease him. Suddenly the Skullbeast rushes at you in a frenzied rage.

Fighting is worked out by means of dice rolls. The Skullbeast has a SKILL of 8. You attack first and also have a SKILL of 8 (unless it has changed earlier in the adventure). Roll two dice. If the total of the two dice is 8 or higher, you slay the Skullbeast. Go to 19A. If the total rolled is 7 or less, the Skullbeast blocks your attack. Roll both dice again, this time for the attack by the Skullbeast. If the total is the same as, or higher than, your SKILL, its blow hits you. Go to 19B. If neither you nor the Skullbeast lands a blow, roll the dice again until either you or the Skullbeast strikes a blow.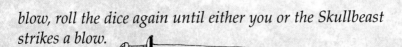

19A If you wish to inspect the Skullbeast's body closely, go to **19E**. If you would rather go back along the main street, go to **12**.

19B The Skullbeast's long claws are razor-sharp, and its vicious swipe catches you on the neck. Reduce your SKILL by 1. You stagger backwards and fall to the ground, and the raging beast closes in for the kill. If you have a Ring of Lightning, go to **19C**. If you do not have this ring, go to **19D**.

19C Just as the Skullbeast is about to strike again, you rub the ring. A bolt of lightning shoots out from the ring and slams into the terrible beast. It drops to the ground like a stone, stopped dead in its tracks. Holding your wounded neck, you must decide what to do. If you want to take a close look at the Skullbeast's body, go to **19E**. If you want to walk back to the main street, go to **12**.

19D As the Skullbeast closes in, you roll out of the way and then jump back up on your feet. Clutching your wounded neck, you ready yourself for battle again. But suddenly the Skullbeast loses interest in you and chases after a young Dwarf who was watching your battle from the safety of a barrel and was foolish enough to climb out. Wasting no time, you leave the alley for the main street. Go to **12**.

19E Your search reveals 6 Gold Pieces, and you put them in your pouch before walking back to the main street. Go to **12**.

20 The first thing about the rooms that amazes you is that they are lit by hundreds of candles. Several paintings of Darkmoon hang on the walls. A large table is the main object in the biggest room, and on it lies a large model of Karazan Castle.

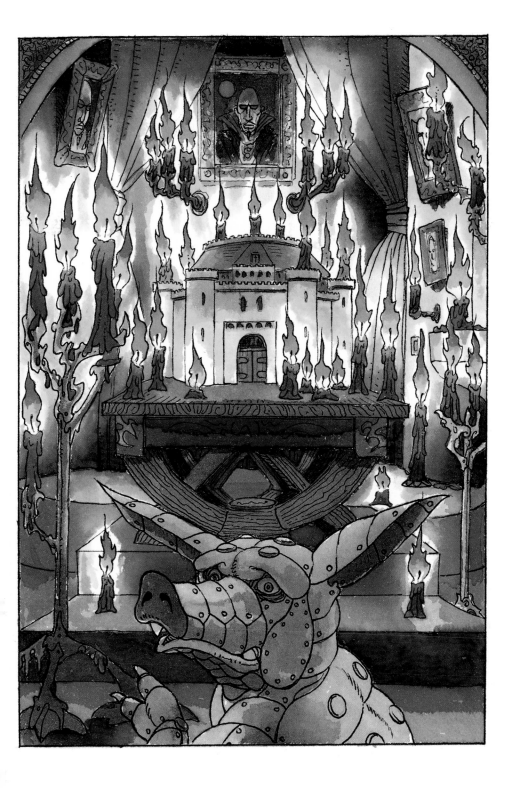

'What mischief is he planning now?' you wonder.

Before Orlando can give his opinion, the roof of the model castle flies up into the air and Darkmoon jumps up, laughing, from inside. His fists are punching the air. You are alarmed to see that he is wearing the ancient crown of Karazan.

'I'm the king of the castle and you're the dirty rascal,' he chants with a wicked grin on his face.

He jumps down off the table and stands in front of you, wagging his black-nailed finger in your face, before resting a thin hand on your shoulder.

'Oh, I'm terrified,' he says mockingly. 'Prince Charming and a fat pig have come to take me away, ha, ha! Don't worry, little piggy, you are about to get a playmate.'

Darkmoon raises his arms and rises to his full height above you, ready to cast a spell. If you are wearing the Golden Hand wristlet, go to **20A**. If you do not have this item, go to **20B**.

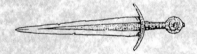

20A You raise your right arm, with the Golden Hand pointing at Darkmoon. His face is suddenly filled with fright and he backs away, trying not to look.

'Take it away! Take it away!' he screams.

'Not a chance,' you reply. 'Give me the crown.'

Darkmoon obeys at once as the magical power of the wristlet begins to drain his own power.

'Now, since you are so good at turning other people into creatures, how about turning my friend here back into a Dwarf,' you say next.

`I can't. The spell won't work backwards,' Darkmoon says with a whimper.

`Then turn yourself into a mouse, or let the power of the Golden Hand destroy you. See how you like your own medicine,' you say, following him around the room.

`All right. I'll do as you command,' Darkmoon agrees. There is a puff of smoke and you watch as a little white mouse scurries away and disappears down a hole in the floorboards. Orlando cheers, and you allow yourself a smile. Go to **21**.

20B Darkmoon mutters a few words and, before you can draw the sword from its scabbard, with a puff of smoke you are changed into a Tin Pig. Darkmoon calls his guards and tells them to throw you and Orlando out of Maggot Manor.

`Winners are grinners,' says Darkmoon with a big smile on his evil face. `Go back to that pigsty you call Karazan Castle and tell the people there that my Orcs will be calling for supper on Tuesday. You lose!'

You have failed in your quest and your adventure is over.

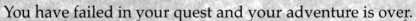

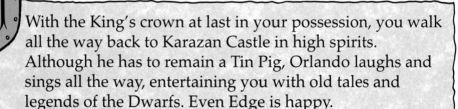

21 With the King's crown at last in your possession, you walk all the way back to Karazan Castle in high spirits. Although he has to remain a Tin Pig, Orlando laughs and sings all the way, entertaining you with old tales and legends of the Dwarfs. Even Edge is happy.

When you get back, the courtyard is packed with all the people who live in the castle. They celebrate your return with trumpets blowing and banners flying, and the noise is deafening. An old man steps out from the crowd and, with a humble smile on his kind face, he shakes you warmly by the hand.

`You did it,' Marris says softly. `I knew you would.'

`Not without Orlando and Edge,' you reply, and your ears are burning at all the fuss. `But how is the real Prince?'

`I can't tell you at the moment,' Marris whispers. `But the news is not good. Let's go inside and talk.'

In the privacy of Marris's library you learn that the Prince is still unconscious and lies hidden in a secret chamber.

`No one else knows, of course,' says Marris. `One royal death is bad enough. And the Orcs still have our armies on the run. What we need is a new King – someone who can take on the Orcs and beat them once and for all.' He pauses, then mutters to himself. `Perhaps ... no, you couldn't possibly.' He stops abruptly. You sense he has more to say, and you press him further.

`Very well, then,' Marris continues. `Would *you* become our King?'

`But what about the real Goldhawk?' you ask.

`Of course, when he recovers, he will take over the crown and you will return to your own world – but until then you will be the King of Karazan!'

Your mind races with excitement. It's a big step, leaving behind the world you know.

`I'll sleep on it,' you say with a smile, although you have already decided what you are going to do.

IAN LIVINGSTONE
ADVENTURES OF GOLDHAWK

THE DEMON SPIDER

Dare you accept the next challenge?